THE GIRL WHO HATED PONIES

Do you love ponies? Be a Pony Pal!

Look for these Pony Pal books:

#1 I Want a Pony

#2 A Pony for Keeps

#3 A Pony in Trouble

#4 Give Me Back My Pony

#5 Pony to the Rescue

#6 Too Many Ponies

#7 Runaway Pony

#8 Good-bye Pony

#9 The Wild Pony

Super Special #1 The Baby Pony

#10 Don't Hurt My Pony

#11 Circus Pony

#12 Keep Out, Pony!

coming soon

#14 Pony-Sitters

THE GIRL WHO HATED PONIES

Jeanne Betancourt

illustrated by Paul Bachem

SCHOLASTIC INC.
New York Toronto London Auckland Sydney

ISBN 0-590-86600-1

24 23 22 21 20 7 8 9/0

Printed in the U.S.A. 40

First Scholastic printing, January 1997

For Felicia La Roche,
a girl who loves ponies

Contents

1

Surprise Company

Lulu Sanders went through the paddock gate and called out her pony's name. Snow White swung around and trotted up to her. Lulu patted her pony's smooth cheek. "We're going to spend the whole weekend riding with our Pony Pals," she told Snow White. Lulu gave Snow White and her stablemate, Acorn, each a carrot. Then she ran into the house for a snack for herself.

Lulu's father was waiting for her in the kitchen. He handed her a mug of hot chocolate and put a plate of cookies on the table. "Thanks, Dad," Lulu said. "What a great surprise."

"I have another surprise for you," her father said.

Lulu looked around the kitchen for a present, but she didn't see any. "What is it?" she asked.

"You know that this weekend I'm going to that wildlife conference on brown bears," Mr. Sanders said. Lulu nodded. "Well, the couple I'm going with have a daughter your age. Her name is Melissa Prince. While we're in Maine, Melissa will stay here. I thought that it would be fun for Melissa to hang out with you and your friends."

"But, Dad," Lulu said, "Anna and I are riding over to Pam's for a sleepover. We're spending the whole weekend with our ponies."

"I'm sure Melissa likes ponies," Lulu's father said. "Her parents both ride."

"Why didn't you tell me this before?" asked Lulu.

"I didn't know Melissa was going to the conference with them," Lulu's father explained. "Playing with you and your friends would be much more fun for her than being in Maine with a bunch of grown-ups."

"I don't know her," protested Lulu. "And what about Pam and Anna? I'm supposed to be with them."

"Don't worry," Mr. Sanders said. "You'll all get along fine. By the end of the weekend there will probably be *four* Pony Pals."

Lulu's father went upstairs for his suitcase. Then Lulu's neighbor, Anna Harley, knocked on the kitchen door. "You ready to ride over to Pam's?" she asked.

"I have to wait for someone," said Lulu. She told Anna the news about Melissa Prince coming for the weekend. "I never met her before," Lulu said. "But my dad invited her for the weekend."

Just then a station wagon pulled into the Sanders' driveway. Lulu and Anna peered out the window. First a man and woman got out of the car. They were both dressed in jeans, hiking boots, and heavy sweaters. A girl wearing a black skirt, lace-up leather boots, and a red jacket climbed out of the backseat. Lulu also noticed that Melissa was wearing long, dangling earrings.

"How old did your father say she was?" asked Anna.

"He said she was our age," Lulu answered.

Melissa's father took her big suitcase from the trunk of the car.

"Do you think she has riding clothes in that suitcase?" asked Anna.

"I sure hope so," said Lulu.

Lulu opened the door for the Princes. Everyone said hello and Lulu and Anna introduced themselves. By then Mr. Sanders had come downstairs and was ready to leave.

“We’d better get moving, Tom,” Mr. Prince told him. “We have a long drive ahead of us.”

Melissa kissed her parents good-bye. “Have a good time, sweetie,” her mother said.

“We’ll be back here to pick you up on Sunday evening around seven,” her father told her. “Have fun.”

Lulu kissed her father good-bye. “I know you’ll take good care of Melissa,” he said. “Show her a good time, be safe, and have a good time yourself.”

“Okay, Dad,” Lulu promised.

The adults left and suddenly Melissa, Anna, and Lulu were left alone in the kitchen.

Melissa smiled at Anna and Lulu. “How old are you guys?” she asked.

“Ten,” answered Anna and Lulu in unison.

“Me too,” said Melissa. She looked around the kitchen. “Your house is pretty.”

“Thanks,” said Lulu. “It’s my grandmother's. She's a hairdresser. She's working up front in her shop."

"Your grandmother is a hairdresser!" exclaimed Melissa. "You're so lucky. You can have your hair done anytime you want."

"I guess," said Lulu. Lulu didn't know what to say next. She had forgotten how hard it was to make friends with someone new. She looked at Anna for some help.

"My mother owns a diner," said Anna. "We go there all the time."

"You're lucky, too," said Melissa. "Let's go to the diner tonight. That would be fun."

"We're having a sleepover tonight," said Lulu. "At our friend Pam Crandal's place. You can come with us. There's plenty of room."

"I love sleepovers," said Melissa happily. She patted her suitcase. "I have my new manicure kit with me. And the neatest nail polish, with gold sparkles. I'll give you all manicures."

Lulu put her hands in her pockets. She didn't want gold sparkles on her fingernails.

"The neatest thing about our sleepovers," Anna told Melissa, "is that we sleep in the barn."

"Doesn't your friend have a house?" Melissa asked with alarm.

Anna and Lulu laughed. "The Crandals have a big house," said Anna.

"Our ponies sleep in the paddock right next to the barn," said Lulu. "All three of us have our own ponies."

"It's fun to sleep in the barn!" exclaimed Anna.

"Sleeping in a barn is *not* my idea of fun," said Melissa. "And I don't like horses."

Lulu's heart sank. She wasn't looking forward to the weekend anymore.

Pony Plop

Lulu walked across the kitchen, picked up the plate of cookies, and held them out. "Want a cookie?" she asked Melissa.

"No thanks," Melissa answered. "Can I see the beauty parlor now?"

"Sure," said Lulu.

"While you do that, I'll go saddle up Acorn and Snow White," said Anna.

Anna left and Lulu and Melissa went through the living room to the beauty parlor.

Grandmother Sanders was cutting a

client's hair. Lulu introduced Melissa and Grandmother to each other. And Grandmother introduced the girls to her client.

Melissa was interested in everything about the beauty parlor. She studied the pictures of hairstyles on the wall. She checked out the colors of nail polish Grandmother kept on her manicurist's table. And she wanted to know what kind of shampoo Grandmother used in her beauty parlor.

"Melissa, my dad said you know how to ride horses," said Lulu.

"I do know how to ride," Melissa answered. "I took riding lessons at summer camp. My parents are always making me ride with them. They love horses. But I don't. Horses and barns smell awful. It's really disgusting."

Grandmother smiled at Melissa. "I agree with you," she said. "But Lulu's pony, Snow White, is special. I love *that* pony."

"I love *every* pony and horse in the whole wide world!" exclaimed Lulu. "And I don't think they smell bad."

“Different people like different things,” said Grandmother. “That’s what makes life interesting.”

“Your grandmother is great,” Melissa whispered to Lulu.

Lulu had an idea. “Grandma, can you drive Melissa over to Pam’s? Anna and I have to ride our ponies there.”

“I’d be glad to give Melissa a ride,” answered Grandmother Sanders. “We’ll go as soon as I finish Mrs. Thompson’s hair and clean up the shop.”

Melissa loved the idea of waiting for Grandmother in the beauty parlor. She sat on one of the chairs and twirled herself around.

“Bye,” said Lulu with a little wave. “I’ll see you at Pam’s.”

Lulu ran out of the shop. She couldn’t get away from Melissa Prince fast enough.

Lulu told Anna what Melissa had said about hating horses. “I think I’m beginning to hate Melissa Prince,” said Anna.

“Me too,” said Lulu.

A few minutes later, Lulu and Anna were riding on Pony Pal Trail. Lulu loved the mile-and-a-half woodland trail that connected Pam's property to Acorn and Snow White's paddock. She moved Snow White into a canter. How could Melissa hate horses? Lulu wondered. She was glad that Pam and Anna loved ponies and the outdoors as much as she did.

Lulu learned a lot about the outdoors and nature from her father. He traveled a lot to study wild animals and Lulu would always go with him. Lulu's mother died when she was little so she was very close to her dad. But when she turned ten, Mr. Sanders decided it was time for Lulu to live in one place. That's why Lulu was living in Wiggins with her grandmother. Lulu loved living in Wiggins where she could have her own pony and be a Pony Pal.

Of all the Pony Pals, Pam Crandal knew the most about ponies. Pam grew up around lots of horses and ponies. Her mother was a riding teacher and her father was a veterinarian. Pam was also the best student in their class at Wiggins Elementary.

Anna Harley was dyslexic and had trouble with reading and math. She enjoyed time *away* from school better than time *in* school. Anna was always ready for an adventure. And she was a great artist. She didn't have her own pony until she was nine years old. But Anna started drawing terrific pictures of ponies when she was really young.

Lulu slowed Snow White down to a trot. I'm lucky to have Anna and Pam for best friends, she thought. I just wish that I didn't have to worry about Melissa Prince all weekend.

Pam and Lightning were waiting for Lulu and Anna in the field at the end of the trail. The three ponies neighed greetings to one another. Acorn and Lightning sniffed noses. While Pam helped Lulu and Anna take off their ponies' saddles and

bridles, Lulu told Pam about Melissa Prince.

"I don't believe she really hates horses," said Pam.

"That's what she said," Lulu told Pam.

"Well, she won't hate them for long," Pam said. She rubbed the upside-down heart of Lightning's forehead. "Who can resist our wonderful ponies?"

"You haven't met Melissa Prince," mumbled Anna.

"Pam is right," said Lulu. "Let's introduce Melissa to our ponies as soon as she gets here."

"It's worth a try," said Anna.

The Pony Pals were walking from the barn to the house when Grandmother's car pulled up the driveway. Melissa got out. Lulu waved to her and yelled, "Melissa come over here."

Melissa said good-bye to Grandmother, picked up her suitcase, and headed across the driveway toward the paddock. Lulu opened the paddock gate and the Pony

Pals came out to meet her. "Hi," said Pam. "I'm Pam Crandal. You can leave your suitcase there. We'll come back for it after."

"After what?" asked Melissa, as she followed the girls into the paddock.

"After you meet our ponies," said Lulu.

Suddenly Melissa jumped back and screeched.

"What happened?" shouted Anna.

Melissa pointed to a pile of pony plop. "I . . . I stepped in *that*!" she cried.

"Sorry," said Pam.

"It's so disgusting," said Melissa. "It's all over my boot!"

"I'll help you clean it off," said Lulu.

"But first come out and meet our ponies," added Anna.

"Your *ponies*!" shouted Melissa. "Is that all you ever think about — your stupid ponies?"

The Pony Pals led Melissa to the barn. Pam looked around for some rubber boots for Melissa to wear in the paddock. Lulu used a scraper on Melissa's soiled leather boot. Anna wiped it with a damp rag.

"A little polish and it will be good as new," said Anna.

Pam handed Melissa the rubber boots.

"Thanks," mumbled Melissa. She looked back at her leather boot. "And thanks for ruining my new boots."

The Pony Pals exchanged a glance. How could they ever turn Melissa Prince into a Pony Pal?

Barn Sleepover

Melissa put on the rubber boots. "Let's go back outside," suggested Pam.

"Forget it," said Melissa. She looked around the barn. "You were joking about sleeping in a barn, right?"

"It's not a joke," said Lulu. "We do sleep in the barn."

"How awful!" exclaimed Melissa. She shivered. "It's cold in here."

"The room we sleep in has a heater," said Pam.

"That's the first good news I've heard

since I came to Wiggins," said Melissa with a little smile.

"Come on, I'll show you the room," said Anna. "It's Mrs. Crandal's office."

"I'll get your suitcase," Lulu said.

"And I'll find you a sleeping bag," added Pam.

A few minutes later the four girls were all in the cozy barn office laying out their sleeping bags.

"This is like sleepaway camp," said Lulu.

"Only we don't have a counselor," said Anna.

"I hated sleepaway camp!" Melissa exclaimed.

Lulu watched out of the corner of her eye as Melissa began to unpack her suitcase. She took out a manicure kit, makeup, a long white nightgown, a very pretty dress, and a pink fluffy bathrobe. "Where can I hang my things?" she asked.

Pam pointed to a hook on the office door. "You can put them there," she said.

"I wish we could go to Anna's restaurant tonight," said Melissa. "Are we going to eat in the barn, too?"

"Sometimes we do," said Pam. "But tonight we're eating in the house. My mother's making spaghetti and meatballs."

"Great," said Melissa.

During dinner, Dr. and Mrs. Crandal asked Melissa questions about her life in New York City. And the six-year-old Crandal twins, Jack and Jill, sang songs from a play they were doing at school. Everyone had a good time and the spaghetti was delicious.

After dinner, Melissa helped with the dishes without being asked. Maybe she's not so bad after all, thought Lulu.

On the way back to the barn the girls stopped at the paddock gate. "Come on," Pam told Melissa. "You can help us feed our ponies."

The three ponies ran across the field toward the girls. "I'll meet you at the barn," said Melissa.

"But you have to meet our ponies," said Pam. "Please."

"Oh, okay," said Melissa. She followed the Pony Pals through the paddock gate. Melissa watched the ground every step she took.

Pam showed Melissa the upside-down heart marking on Lightning's forehead. "That's neat," said Melissa.

"Rub it," said Pam. "It's softer than the rest of her coat."

Melissa put her hands behind her back. "Another time," she said.

Lulu patted Snow White on the neck. "And this is Snow White," she said. "She's grown her winter coat, so she's fuzzy now. But in the summer she's shiny." Snow White took a few steps toward Melissa and nickered as if to say hello. Melissa moved away from Snow White and didn't say hello back.

Anna hugged her cute brown-and-black Shetland pony. "And this is Acorn," she said proudly.

"Acorn knows tricks," said Lulu.

"He and Anna were in the circus," added Pam. "They were great."

"Watch this," said Anna. "Acorn, do you like Melissa?" she asked.

Acorn nodded his head yes.

Everyone clapped. But Melissa didn't touch Acorn or say that he was a special pony.

"Come on, Melissa," Pam said. "Help us feed them."

"I'm going back to the office," Melissa told the Pony Pals. "I want to write in my diary."

Lulu had a feeling that Melissa wasn't going to have anything nice to say about them, or their ponies, in her diary.

After the Pony Pals fed their ponies, they went to the barn office. Melissa was sitting at Mrs. Crandal's desk. She had on her pink bathrobe and was writing in her diary. She closed it when they came in and snapped the lock shut.

"You know what I don't understand?" Melissa said.

"What?" asked the Pony Pals in unison.

"I don't understand why people have horses anymore," she answered. "We don't need horses for transportation. We have cars, trains, and planes."

"Horses are beautiful and wonderful," said Lulu. "That's a good enough reason to have them."

"Besides," said Anna. "We're too young to drive a car."

"Ride a bicycle then," said Melissa. "They make these great mountain bikes now. You can ride them anywhere."

"I'd rather have Snow White than a bike," protested Lulu.

"But you don't have to feed a bike," argued Melissa. "And they don't drop plops of you-know-what everywhere."

The Pony Pals exchanged a glance and silently agreed not to argue with Melissa.

"Different people like different things," Lulu said. "That's what my grandmother always says."

"I have an idea," said Melissa. "Tomorrow, let's go back to Lulu's and do makeovers." She smiled at Lulu. "Lulu, you'd look great with curls. Your grandmother has curlers that would work perfect on your hair."

Lulu ran her fingers though her straight hair. "I like my hair the way it is," she said.

Melissa ignored her. She was smiling at Pam now. "I have the perfect nail polish for you, Pam. By the way, you have great long legs. You should always wear miniskirts. You can borrow mine."

"You can't ride a horse in a miniskirt," mumbled Pam.

Now Melissa was smiling at Anna. "Anna," she said, "I think a different hairstyle would make you look older."

"Why would I want to look older?" asked Anna.

Melissa laughed and looked around at the Pony Pals. "You three," she said. "I can see I have my work cut out for me here. But after the makeovers you'll be known as the *Pretty* Pals instead of the Pony Pals."

Anna rolled her eyes. Pam covered her mouth so she wouldn't laugh out loud. And Lulu shook her head in wonder. How would they ever get through a weekend with Melissa Prince?

Riding Lesson

Lulu was the first to wake up the next morning. She waited quietly until Anna and Pam opened their eyes. But Melissa was still sound asleep. Lulu signaled Anna and Pam to be quiet and go outside.

Soon the three girls were dressed and feeding their ponies. Lulu looked up at the clear sky. "It's going to be a beautiful day," she said. "Perfect for trail riding."

"Or for *makeovers*," joked Anna.

"Never!" said Lulu. "I don't want curls in my hair."

"Don't you want to be a *Pretty* Pal?" asked Pam with a laugh.

"We have to keep Melissa so busy today that she forgets all about makeovers," said Anna.

"We could take her on a long trail ride," suggested Pam.

"She said she knows how to ride," said Lulu.

"Let's see if my mother can spare one of her school ponies," suggested Pam.

The girls ran to the house. Mrs. Crandal was in the kitchen eating breakfast. "Where's Melissa?" she asked.

"She's still sleeping," said Lulu.

Pam asked her mother if they could borrow a pony for Melissa.

Mrs. Crandal thought for a second. "I'm not using Splash today," she said. "You could borrow him. But I'll have to check out Melissa's riding skills." She looked at her watch. "Bring her to the ring at nine o'clock. I'll fit her in before my first lesson."

"Thanks, Mom," said Pam.

"You three be ready to ride, too," said Mrs. Crandal. "I have to know that Melissa can handle a pony in a group situation."

Anna and Lulu wrapped some hot muffins in paper napkins. Pam found four bananas, a quart of orange juice, and four paper cups. They put every thing in a wicker basket and took it to the barn. "Morning, Melissa," Lulu called as they came into the office.

"We're all going to have breakfast in bed," announced Anna.

Melissa sat up and smiled at them. "It smells great," she said.

The four girls sat on their sleeping bags and ate.

"When are we going back to Lulu's?" asked Melissa.

"After we go trail riding," said Lulu. Then she explained to Melissa about Splash and the riding lesson.

"I told you I want to do makeovers today," said Melissa. "I don't want to ride."

"But *we* don't want to do makeovers," said Lulu.

The two girls stared at one another.

"Melissa, you said you could ride," said Pam. "If you can't that's all right. We can do something else."

"I *can* ride," said Melissa.

"Then prove it," said Lulu. "Ride with us in the ring."

"And then we can all go trail riding together," said Anna. "It will be fun. You'll see."

Melissa thought for a second. "I'll make a deal with you," she said. "I'll ride with you today, if you do makeovers with me tomorrow."

The Pony Pals looked at one another, hesitated for a second, and nodded.

"Okay," Lulu told Melissa. "It's a deal."

Half an hour later the Pony Pals, their ponies, and Melissa went to the riding ring.

Mrs. Crandal led Splash into the circle. She told Melissa to come in the ring, too. "You three wait outside the fence for now," Mrs. Crandal called to the Pony Pals.

They watched as Melissa mounted Splash. Mrs. Crandal directed her to walk the pony around the ring. Then she had her move Splash into a trot. Next, she checked that Melissa could stop and start Splash. "Good work, Melissa," Mrs. Crandal said.

"Okay, girls," Mrs. Crandal called to the Pony Pals. "Mount and ride around the ring with Melissa."

The four girls rode their ponies around the ring in a walk, trot, and canter. They made turns and cut across the ring. Melissa seemed to know what she was doing. Maybe we'll have fun today, after all, Lulu thought.

Mrs. Crandal said that Melissa could go out on the trails with Splash. "Where are you girls riding today?" she asked.

"On the trails near Mount Morris," answered Pam.

"Stick to the easy trails," Mrs. Crandal told them. "Melissa hasn't had as much experience trail riding as you girls."

The girls packed their lunch and carrots for the ponies. They were finally ready to begin the trail ride. It was Pam's turn to take the lead. Then came Anna and Acorn, followed by Melissa and Splash. Lulu and Snow White took up the rear.

The riders crossed Riddle Road and went onto the first trail. After a few minutes on the trail, Splash stumbled and lurched forward. Melissa let out a little scream, but didn't fall out of the saddle. Splash regained his footing and moved back into a trot.

Lulu rode up beside Melissa. "He just

slipped on a rock," she told her. "It happens when you trail ride."

"I know," grumbled Melissa.

Lulu had a feeling that Melissa Prince wouldn't have much fun on the trail ride after all.

Snow White's New Rider

Lulu wasn't having fun on the trail ride, either. Melissa complained about everything. She said Splash was a bumpy trotter and that it was too cold to ride. Melissa even said she wished she'd never come to Wiggins. Lulu wished Melissa Prince had never come to Wiggins, too. Especially when Melissa kept saying, "This is *so* boring."

Suddenly Splash ran ahead, passed Acorn, and almost bumped into Lightning. "Whoa!" Melissa called out.

Splash stopped and neighed as if to say, "Are you bored now?"

The other riders halted their ponies.

"Splash used to rush the other ponies like that all the time," Anna explained to Melissa. "We had to train him to behave on the trail."

"Well, you didn't do a very good job!" said Melissa.

"We did too," Anna said. Anna and Melissa glared at each other.

"We can't let Splash get away with that kind of behavior," said Lulu.

"Maybe one of us should ride him," suggested Pam. "Otherwise he'll be a problem pony for my mother."

"I'll do it," said Lulu. "Melissa can ride Snow White."

"I hope Snow White behaves," said Melissa.

Lulu wanted to say, *Snow White behaves a lot better than* you *do.* But she didn't.

Lulu dismounted Snow White. She patted her pony on the cheek and whispered in her ear. "Melissa is going to ride you for a little while."

Melissa mounted Snow White and Lulu mounted Splash. At first Lulu had to give all her attention to Splash. Finally, Splash understood that he had to cooperate with her. Lulu looked ahead to see how Melissa was doing with Snow White. She didn't like the way Melissa was treating Snow White.

"Melissa, Snow White has a soft mouth," Lulu shouted. "Don't rein her so hard."

A minute later Lulu called to Melissa. "You don't have to kick Snow White to move her into a trot. Just shift your body a little."

Melissa turned around in the saddle. "I'm not going to hurt your precious pony," she said.

"Pay attention to your riding and stop turning around," Lulu yelled.

"I hate trail riding!" shouted Melissa. "I hate horses!"

Lulu rode past Melissa and up to Anna and Pam. "I'll bring Melissa back to Pam's," she whispered. "She's ruining the ride for everyone. It's not fair to you guys."

"She's not being fair to you," said Pam.

"She's my company," Lulu said. "So she's my problem."

"Your problem is our problem," said Pam.

"Melissa is just another Pony Pal Problem," whispered Anna.

"Let's stop for lunch now," suggested Pam. "That might put her in a better mood."

Melissa rode up to them. "What's the big secret?" she asked.

"We're deciding where to eat lunch," said Anna.

Pam pointed ahead. "Let's stop on the other side of that hill. There's a stream where the ponies can drink."

Soon the ponies were drinking from the stream and the girls sat on a big rock to eat lunch. Pam opened the thermos of tomato soup and poured some for each of them. Lulu handed out sandwiches.

"Saturdays my friends and I always go for pizza," said Melissa. "We sit in booths in a *warm* pizza parlor."

"Goody for you," mumbled Anna. Anna and Melissa exchanged an angry glance.

Just then, Snow White whinnied in an upset tone. Lulu ran over and stroked her mane. "What's wrong, Snow White?" she asked.

Pam stood up to look around at what might have upset the pony. "It's starting to snow," she said.

Lulu looked up. The sun was blocked by huge dark clouds that were filling the sky.

"It's snowing," said Melissa.

Lulu felt the first flakes on her face. Snow White nickered nervously. "It's okay,

Snow White," she told her pony. "We'll get going."

By the time they had packed up their lunches the sky was totally dark and the air was swirling with snow.

"Why did we go trail riding if it was going to snow?" asked Melissa.

"The weather report this morning didn't say anything about snow," said Pam.

Snow White snorted and pranced in place, her ears forward. Splash snorted, too. And Lightning pulled on her lead rope. The girls tried to calm the ponies down.

What's going on? Lulu wondered. Why is Snow White so upset by the storm?

The snow swirled around the girls and their ponies. Lulu couldn't see more than a foot in front of her. She had to shout to be heard above the wind.

We are in a dangerous situation, Lulu told herself. So I have to stay calm. Pam and Anna were staying calm, too. But Melissa was shivering with cold and fear. Lulu knew that both her pony and Melissa were very frightened. And even though she didn't show it, Lulu was scared, too.

Afraid!

The four girls stood near the ponies. They were ready to leave, but Lulu wasn't sure they could find their way home in the blinding snowstorm.

"We'd better not try to go back yet," said Pam.

"Right," Anna agreed.

"We have to go back," yelled Melissa. "We'll freeze to death out here!"

"We'll be all right, Melissa," Lulu said. "We'll take cover until the storm calms down. Then we'll go back to Pam's."

"What if it doesn't calm down?" asked Melissa in a panicky voice. "What if it goes on for days and days?"

"We're going to be all right," Lulu told Melissa again. "You have to believe me." Lulu wished she believed herself.

"Let's think of where we can go to get some cover," said Anna.

"There's a wooden shelter on this side of the hill," said Pam. "Campers use it."

"It's not far from here," said Anna. "But I don't know how to find it."

"I think it's to our right," said Pam.

"The ponies are scared," said Melissa. "Maybe we should just let them go."

Lulu held tight to Snow White's reins. "That's a terrible idea," she told Melissa.

"We'll walk and lead the ponies," said Pam. "I'll go first with Lightning."

"I'll follow with Snow White and Splash," said Lulu. "Melissa you walk beside me. Anna, you follow with Acorn."

"Let's use our whistles," suggested Anna.

"What whistles?" asked Melissa.

"We have whistles for when we go on trail rides," Anna explained to Melissa. "Lulu's father gave them to us when we went on our first overnight camping trip."

"If you lose sight of the person in front of you, blow your whistle once," said Lulu. "Wait five seconds, then blow it again. Do that until we find you."

"If I find the shelter, I'll blow two short blasts," said Pam.

"I don't have a whistle," said Melissa fearfully. "What if I get lost?"

Lulu took her whistle off and put it around Melissa's neck. "Stay right next to me," Lulu told her. "You have the whistle. I'm depending on you."

The girls and ponies moved slowly through the storm. Snow pricked Lulu's face like a thousand needles. She could barely see her white pony in the swirl of snow. But she could feel Snow White's breath on her and she knew that Snow White was still nervous. If we find the shelter, she thought, I'll keep Snow White in there with me until she's calm again.

Lulu heard a whistle blast, then another. "Pam found the shelter," Lulu told Snow White.

Snow White nuzzled Lulu's shoulder. "Everything will be okay," she told her pony.

Because of the swirling snow, Lulu couldn't see the shelter until they were right in front of it. It had a wooden floor, three sides, and a roof.

"There are plenty of trees we can use for hitching up the ponies," Pam yelled above the roar of the wind.

"Let's tie them up and go inside," shouted Anna.

Loosening the ponies' girths and tying them to the trees was hard work in the storm. "Melissa, loosen Splash's girth," Lulu yelled.

"I can't," said Melissa. "I'm too cold."

We have enough problems with this storm, Lulu thought, without having to

worry about Melissa. Lulu was trying not to be angry at Melissa. But it was hard.

They tied Acorn, Lightning, and Splash under trees near the wooden shelter. "They're strong ponies," said Pam. "They've all been in bad weather before. They'll be all right." Lulu remembered how Snow White was lost in a snowstorm and fell in an icy hole. That's probably why she's upset by this storm, Lulu thought.

"We're lucky that the wind isn't blowing into the open side of the shelter," said Anna.

Melissa went to the farthest corner of the shelter and sat down. Lulu led Snow White in. "Come on," she told her pony soothingly. "I'll brush you off."

Melissa leaped to her feet. "Leave her outside with the other ponies," she shouted.

"She's frightened," Lulu told Melissa. "I need to calm her down."

"If you're bringing the horses in here,

I'm leaving," shouted Melissa. She moved quickly toward the edge of the shelter.

"Wait!" shouted Lulu. Anna grabbed Melissa's arm. Pam stood in front of her.

Melissa tried to pull away from Anna. Pam grabbed her other arm.

"You can't go out in that storm alone," shouted Pam. "You'll get lost!"

Lightning whinnied when she heard the shouting. Snow White pranced in place.

"I'm not going to stay here to be trampled by horses," shouted Melissa.

Lulu was angry at Melissa. But she was also responsible for her. She had promised her father. She'd brought this city girl on a trail ride that had turned dangerous. No matter what, she had to take care of Melissa and be sure that she was safe.

"As soon as Snow White is calm, I'll put her outside with the other ponies," said Lulu.

Finally, Melissa went back to the corner and sat down again. But Lulu knew she might try to run out in the snowstorm again.

The Pony Pals needed to talk about the problem they were having with Melissa. But they couldn't talk in front of her and they couldn't leave her alone. They needed to solve this problem before Melissa did something else that was crazy. Something that would put them all in danger.

Secret Notes

Pam turned away from Melissa and took a small notebook out of her jacket pocket. She quickly wrote something. When Melissa wasn't looking, Pam secretly passed the notebook to Lulu.

I think Melissa hates ponies because she's afraid of them.

After Lulu read Pam's idea she gave the notebook to Anna. Anna read what Pam wrote. Then she wrote something herself.

Anna handed the pad back to Pam. Pam read Anna's idea and handed it to Lulu. Pam and Anna petted Snow White while Lulu read Anna's idea.

Ask M. why she is afraid of ~~*~~ horses.

Lulu wrote down her idea and secretly showed it to Pam and Anna.

Let's try being nice to her.

Lulu could see Melissa crouched in the corner. She looked sad and scared. The Pony Pals went over to Melissa and sat down beside her. Pam was the first to speak. She pointed to Snow White. The pony was standing calmly now. "Snow White isn't upset anymore," Pam said.

"She was probably spooked because she got lost in a snowstorm once and fell in an icy hole," said Lulu. Then the Pony Pals told Melissa how Snow White had run away and how they saved her.

"See, Melissa, we've been in trouble before," Pam said. "But we always work it out."

Anna put a hand on Melissa's arm. "Everything will be fine as long as we stick together," she said.

Melissa looked around at the Pony Pals. "I told you I hate horses," she said. "I shouldn't have come with you."

"Everyone has things they hate," said Pam. "I've hated snakes forever. Snakes really scare me. I know the snakes around here are harmless, but they still scare me."

The strong wind blew through the shelter. Melissa moved over so the Pony Pals could fit in the corner, too.

"How come you're so scared of snakes?" Melissa asked Pam.

"I think it's because of what Tommy Rand did to me when I was little," Pam answered.

"Tommy Rand is this tough-acting older kid at our school," Lulu explained to Melissa.

"He can be really obnoxious," added Anna.

"What'd he do to you?" Melissa asked Pam.

"His mother came to see my mother about something," Pam said. "It was the first time I met him. I was only about four years old."

"So he must have been around seven," said Anna.

"Our mothers told us to play outside," Pam continued. "Tommy was chasing me, when something landed across my shoulders. Tommy shouted, *'Watch out! That snake is going to bite you!'* I looked down and saw that a huge snake was wrapped around my neck. I screamed."

"That would scare *anyone*," said Lulu.

"I was terrified," said Pam with a shudder. "Even when I realized that Tommy had put a dead snake on me. After that I started having nightmares about snakes. Sometimes I still do."

"I have nightmares about horses," Melissa whispered.

"Maybe you hate horses because you're afraid of them," Lulu said.

"Maybe," said Melissa.

"Did horses scare you when you were little?" Anna asked Melissa.

Melissa looked over at Snow White. Lulu saw a frightened look in her eyes. Melissa moved farther back into the corner. "I just remembered what happened to me when I was little," she said.

"Tell us," said Anna.

Melissa hid her head in her arms and didn't answer.

The wind blew a gust of snow into the shelter. Lulu shivered from the cold. She could barely make out the shapes of the three ponies in the swirling snow. How long would it be before the snowstorm ended?

Lost in a Barn

The storm was so bad that snow blew into the girls' faces. Melissa looked up. "The storm's getting worse," she said.

"Don't worry," Lulu told Melissa. "It will end soon." The Pony Pals exchanged a glance. They all knew that surprise storms could last a very long time.

"Melissa, was it one horse that scared you or a lot of them?" asked Pam.

"One," answered Melissa.

"How old were you?" asked Anna.

"I was really little," said Melissa.

"Where were you?" asked Pam.

"In a big horse barn with my parents," answered Melissa. "I must have wandered off by myself. I remember being alone. I was walking on straw and kicking it with my feet."

"If there was straw on the floor, you probably were in a stall," said Lulu.

"You were so little. I bet you walked right under the stall guard without noticing it," added Pam.

"I guess," said Melissa. "When I looked up, there was a huge horse standing over me. That horse looked so big to me. I was too afraid to move or to yell for help. So I just sat down on the straw." Melissa looked around her. "I was in a corner like this one," she said with a shudder.

"What happened next?" asked Anna.

"The horse pawed the ground and made scary noises," Melissa answered.

"It was probably snorting," said Pam.

"Then it came over and sniffed me," said Melissa.

Lulu imagined a little child being sniffed by a big horse that terrified her. "How scary!" she exclaimed.

"I thought that horse was going to eat me up," said Melissa.

"No wonder you don't like horses," said Anna.

"And have nightmares about them," added Pam.

The Pony Pals exchanged a glance. Now they knew why Melissa hated horses.

"What happened next?" asked Lulu. "How did you get out?"

Melissa thought for a second. "I don't know," she said. "I remember that I was too afraid to cry for help. I suppose my parents found me. I guess that's the day I started hating horses."

"That's just like me and snakes," said Pam. "I say I hate them, but I only hate them because I'm afraid of them."

Just then Snow White took a step toward the girls. Melissa jumped up and moved away from the pony.

Snow White nickered gently, as if to say, "Don't be afraid of me. I'm your friend."

"Snow White would never hurt you, Melissa," Lulu said. "You can trust her."

"Why don't you pet her?" suggested Anna.

Melissa paused a moment and then reached out and put her hand on Snow White's neck. Snow White nickered again and lowered her head for more attention. Melissa stroked her neck. "You're a good pony, Snow White," Melissa said. "You don't have to be afraid of the snow. We'll take care of you."

"I'll put Snow White outside," said Lulu. "She's calm now and it will give us more room in here."

Lulu led Snow White out of the shelter and tied her to a tree. Acorn looked up and nickered at his friend, as if to say, "Glad to see you." Lulu felt the snow swirling around her. She still couldn't see more than a foot in front of her. It was a really bad storm. Melissa wasn't a problem any-

more. But now they had an even bigger problem to solve. How would they stay safe until the surprise snowstorm ended?

Lulu went back into the shelter. "We have to do something to keep warm," she told the others.

"Let's build a fire," suggested Melissa.

"All the wood is wet," said Pam.

"Besides," added Lulu, "we can't build a fire in the shelter. We might burn it down."

"We should move around to keep warm," said Pam.

"But we shouldn't use up a lot of energy," said Lulu. "There's no food left and only a little water."

"I can teach you a line dance," suggested Melissa.

"Perfect," said Anna.

Pam and Lulu liked the idea, too.

"Line up beside me," Melissa directed.

Lulu stood on one side of Melissa and Anna and Pam on the other.

"Now, take two steps to the left," Melissa told them.

They did it.

"Now, we all step forward on our right foot and kick out our left foot," she instructed.

Anna started to step forward with her left foot, but Pam gave her a little nudge and she changed feet.

In a few minutes they knew Melissa's line dance. They did it a few times.

Next, they played Simon Says . . .

They were having fun and laughing a lot. But Lulu knew they were still in danger. We're caught in a snowstorm a long way from home, she thought. She checked her watch. It was four o'clock. Soon it would be dark. What will we do to stay warm if the storm keeps up all night? she wondered.

"I'm tired," Anna said. "Let's rest for awhile."

"It's getting colder," said Pam. "We have to keep moving."

"I wish it would stop snowing," said Melissa.

Lulu stood on the edge of the shelter and looked out. She could see the outline of the treetops. "I think it's stopping," she said.

"I hope you're right," said Anna.

Lulu was right. In a few minutes the snow and wind stopped completely. The girls could clearly see the woods around them. They hit high fives and shouted, "All *right*!" The ponies whinnied.

Lulu stepped out of the shelter onto the snow-covered ground. "It's only a couple of inches," she said. "The ponies can get through it fine."

"But which way did we come from?" asked Pam.

Lulu looked around her. She had never ridden in this part of the woods before. She didn't know the way back to the Crandals'.

Pam pointed to the space between two big pine trees. "I think it's that way," she said.

Anna pointed straight ahead of them.

"Or maybe it was that way," she suggested.

"It's hard to remember because we couldn't see anything when we got here," said Pam.

The Pony Pals exchanged a glance. None of them was sure of the way out of the woods. They had never been lost before. How could they get home?

S.O.S.

Lulu looked over at Melissa. She hoped she wouldn't act nervous and scared again. But Melissa was dealing with the problem as calmly as the Pony Pals. "We won't get too lost in either direction," she said. "We can find our way back here by following the footprints we make in the snow. Then we can try another way."

"Good thinking, Melissa," said Pam.

"Let's try Pam's way first," said Anna. "She's the one who led us here."

"We'd better hurry," said Lulu. "It'll be dark soon and then we won't be able to see anything. Even our own footprints."

"And it's dangerous to ride in the dark," said Pam.

"It's more dangerous to have to stay overnight in the woods without thermal sleeping bags," said Lulu.

"However you look at it," Anna said, "we'd better move fast."

The girls quickly dusted snow off the saddles and tightened the ponies' girths. Lulu checked her watch again. It was five o'clock. In half an hour it would be dark. "Melissa, if we all go on horseback, we can move faster," Lulu said. "Do you think you can ride?"

Melissa nodded. "I'll be okay," she said.

"You take Snow White," said Lulu, "and I'll take Splash."

Lulu mounted Splash. Melissa pulled down Snow White's stirrups and mounted. "Thanks for being so nice to me," Melissa

told Lulu. "I'm not so scared now that I talked about what happened when I was little."

Lulu was glad that Melissa said thank you. But she couldn't spend any time thinking about that. They were all in danger. And they needed to find the way out of the cold woods before nightfall.

After about ten minutes of riding, Pam halted Lightning and turned in the saddle. "I don't think this is the right way," she shouted back to the others. "It's all brush ahead of us. The trail ends. We'd better go back."

The four riders turned their ponies around. Now Lulu and Splash were in the lead. Lulu was cold and wished she had worn her long underwear. How could they survive the night? They needed help to get out of the woods. That's when Lulu thought of the whistles. "Everybody stop!" she yelled. "Maybe someone is out looking for us. Let's use our whistles to let them know where we are."

Pam and Anna rode up beside Lulu and Melissa. Melissa handed Lulu back her whistle. “You should all blow together,” she said. “It will be louder that way.”

“Good idea,” said Anna.

“On the count of four, then,” said Melissa. Melissa counted one-two-three-four. Then the Pony Pals blew the S.O.S. signal. One short blast, a long one, and another short one.

They waited and listened. Then they blew the S.O.S. again.

There was no answer to their call for help. “Let’s ride a little ways and try again,” said Lulu.

They rode, stopped to blow the S.O.S. signal, and listened. This time Lulu thought she heard something. “It was like a humming sound,” she told the others.

But no one else had heard it.

“Try again,” Lulu told them.

“One-two-three-four,” said Melissa.

“*Wheet*! *Whee-ee-eet*! *Wheet*!” blew the whistles.

The girls listened. “I heard something that time,” said Anna.

“Me too,” said Pam.

“It's a humming sound,” said Melissa. “But from far away.”

The girls put their whistles to their lips and blew with all their might. And listened.

“It's coming closer to us,” said Pam. “We have to keep blowing.”

The girls blew their S.O.S. signal over and over again.

Each time they stopped to catch their breath, the humming sound was closer.

“I bet it's a snowmobile!” shouted Pam.

“I hope it's someone who will help us,” said Lulu.

They blew their signal again. Soon, out of the darkness, Lulu saw two bright lights. “Hello there,” shouted a man's voice.

“It's my father!” shouted Pam.

“Pam!” shouted Dr. Crandal.

All the ponies except Acorn were

spooked by the noise and bright lights of the snowmobile. Dr. Crandal turned it around so the lights wouldn't shine in their eyes.

"It's only me, ponies," Dr. Crandal called out. When the ponies heard Dr. Crandal's familiar voice they calmed down. "Thank goodness I found you girls," he said. "Is everybody okay?"

"We're cold," said Anna.

"And hungry," said Lulu.

"But otherwise we're fine," said Melissa.

"We were sort of lost," Pam told her father. "But we found a place to stay out of the storm."

"And how are the ponies?" asked Dr. Crandal. He rubbed a hand over Lightning's neck.

Lulu patted Splash. "Splash is okay," she said.

The other girls said that their ponies were fine, too.

Dr. Crandal stepped over to Melissa, who was still mounted on Snow White.

"How are you doing, Melissa?" he said. "I don't expect you have adventures like this in New York City."

"I'm okay," said Melissa. "The Pony Pals took good care of me."

"Why don't you ride back with me in the snowmobile," he said. "Lulu can trail Snow White behind Splash."

Melissa shook her head. "I want to ride with the Pony Pals," she said. She patted Snow White on the neck. "It's not every day I have a chance to ride a pony as wonderful as Snow White."

"Melissa is turning into a Pony Pal after all," Pam whispered to Lulu.

"We'll still have to do makeovers with her tomorrow," said Lulu.

"I forgot about the makeovers!" said Pam.

"I bet Melissa didn't forget," said Lulu with a giggle.

Pam and Lulu moved into line behind Anna and Melissa. The snowmobile lit up the way for the line of riders. Lulu was happy that they were safe and that soon they'd be back at the Crandals'. But she didn't want to spend the whole next day in her grandmother's beauty parlor. She didn't want curly hair. And she didn't want gold sparkles on her nails, either. *We made a deal with Melissa,* thought Lulu. *Tomorrow the Pony Pals will become the Pretty Pals.*

Makeovers

That night Melissa and the Pony Pals had another barn sleepover. Before they went to sleep they made a plan for their Makeover Day.

"Let's stop at the diner and have breakfast on the way," said Anna.

"Terrific," said Melissa. "I want to go to your mother's diner."

"Anna and I will have to ride to the diner," said Lulu. "Our ponies are here."

"Can't we all ride?" asked Melissa.

"Sure!" said Pam. "The ponies can be

together in Acorn and Snow White's paddock. They'll like that."

"You can ride Snow White," Lulu told Melissa. "And I'll ride Splash."

"Thanks," said Melissa. "I'll do your manicure first."

Lulu tried to smile when she said thanks.

The next morning was sunny. All of Wiggins sparkled under the blanket of snow left by the sudden storm. The girls fed the ponies and saddled them up for the ride to the diner. Splash whinnied happily when he saw that he was going on another ride with the Pony Pals and their ponies. "Splash likes being a Pony Pal," said Anna.

"Me too," said Melissa.

Lulu rode behind Melissa. She didn't have any complaints about how Melissa rode Snow White. Melissa was relaxed in the saddle. She didn't pull on Snow White's mouth and she didn't kick him. Everyone enjoyed the ride to the diner.

The four girls tied the ponies to the hitching post and went inside.

"We always try to sit in the last booth," Anna explained to Melissa. "It's our favorite and we can see the ponies from there."

"And we are our own waiters," said Pam.

The girls all had orange juice and blueberry pancakes. While they ate they talked about the adventure they had in the woods the day before. They laughed when they remembered how they learned a line dance and played Simon Says . . . in the middle of a blizzard. I like being with Melissa now, thought Lulu. I just wish she wasn't going to curl my hair and put gold sparkles on my nails.

Melissa looked out the window at the ponies. "It isn't fair," she said. "The ponies were in the blizzard, too. But we're having all the fun. Can I bring them a treat?"

"You can take apples from the kitchen for them," said Anna.

"Come on Melissa," said Lulu. "I'll go with you."

"Pam and I will get *us* some more food," said Anna.

Melissa and Lulu brought apples out to the ponies. Melissa gave the first one to Snow White. "Look how matted Snow White's mane is," she said with a frown. "She could use a good brushing."

Lulu put her hand out with an apple for Acorn. "Acorn's whiskers should be trimmed," she said. "And the fuzz in his ears needs trimming, too."

Melissa rubbed Lightning's upside-down heart.

"Lightning's marking shines when we rub a little oil in it," Lulu told her.

"That would be so pretty," said Melissa.

When the apples were gone they went back in the diner. Anna and Pam were sitting in the booth waiting for them. At each place there was a dish of sliced strawberries and bananas topped with yogurt. Anna held up a take-out bag. "We can have a brownie break while we're doing the makeovers," she said.

"The brownies from Off-Main Diner are the best," Lulu told Melissa.

"I have an idea," said Melissa. "Instead of giving one another makeovers, why don't we give the ponies makeovers. They could really use it."

"Are you sure?" Anna asked.

Melissa looked around at the Pony Pals. "You guys don't need makeovers," she said. "You look pretty good just the way you are."

"Pony Makeovers," said Lulu. "It's a great idea."

"Lightning loves to be groomed," said Pam. "She'll be so happy."

"Let's make a list of all the things we'll do for them," said Anna. "Then we can check off each thing as we do it. Otherwise, we might lose track."

"We'll do Splash, too," said Lulu.

Pam took out her pocket notebook and

the girls made the checklist for the Pony Makeovers.

Pony Makeovers

	S.W.	Ltng.	Acorn	Splash
• TRIM				
1) whiskers on nose				
2) fuzz in ears				
3) fetlocks and legs				
4) tails				
• CURRY COATS				
• BRUSH manes and tails				
• RUB baby oil on nose, tips of ears, and Lightning's upside down heart				
• POLISH hooves with hoof oil				
• RUB coats				
• BRAID manes				

"I brought my camera," said Melissa. "We'll take before and after pictures, just like they do in the magazines." She stood up. "Let's go. I can't wait to get started."

The first thing the four girls did for the makeover was take *before* pictures of the ponies. Then they lined up all of their supplies. Each girl took a pony. After the ponies were groomed, the girls put braids and ribbons in their manes.

Melissa stood back and admired Snow White. "She looks wonderful," she said. "Okay, let's take *after* pictures."

"Why don't you stand next to Snow White," Lulu told Melissa, "and I'll take your picture."

"It'll be your souvenir," said Anna.

"Of your weekend as a Pony Pal," Pam added.

Melissa looked at her reflection in the window and laughed. Her clothes were wrinkled and dusty from riding and grooming Snow White. Her hairdo was crushed by a baseball cap and she had a smear of dirt across one cheek. "I'm a

mess," she said. "But Snow White looks great." Melissa gave Snow White a hug. "Go ahead," she told Lulu. "Take our picture."

Snow White nuzzled Melissa's shoulder. Lulu thought that Melissa looked prettier and happier than she did when she was dressed in a fancy outfit and had painted nails. Best of all, Lulu knew that Melissa didn't hate horses anymore. Lulu was proud of her pony and her new friend.

Dear Reader,

I am having a lot of fun researching and writing books about the Pony Pals. I've met many interesting kids and adults who love ponies. And I've visited some wonderful ponies at homes, farms, and riding schools.

Before writing Pony Pals I wrote fourteen novels for children and young adults. Four of these were honored by Children's Choice Awards.

I live in Sharon, Connecticut, with my husband, Lee, and our dog, Willie. Our daughter is all grown up and has her own apartment in New York City.

Besides writing novels I like to draw, paint, garden and swim. I didn't have a pony when I was growing up, but I have always loved them and dreamt about riding. Now I take riding lessons on a horse named Saz. To learn more, visit my Web site: www.jeannebetancourt.com.

I like reading and writing about ponies as much as I do riding. Which proves to me that you don't have to ride a pony to love them. And you certainly don't need a pony to be a Pony Pal.

Happy Reading,

Jeanne Betancourt